The Really Groovy Story of the Tortoise and the Hare

Kristyn Crow   illustrated by Christina Forshay

FICTION READALONG
AV2
BY WEIGL™
ADDED VALUE • AUDIO VISUAL

www.av2books.com

Your AV² Media Enhanced book gives you a fiction readalong online. Log on to www.av2books.com and enter the unique book code from this page to use your readalong.

AV² Readalong Navigation

Go to **www.av2books.com**, and enter this book's unique code.

BOOK CODE

L574935

AV² by Weigl brings you media enhanced books that support active learning.

First Published by

ALBERT WHITMAN & COMPANY
Publishing children's books since 1919

HIGHLIGHTED TEXT

HOME

START READING

CLOSE

TITLE INFORMATION

PAGE TURNING

PAGE PREVIEW

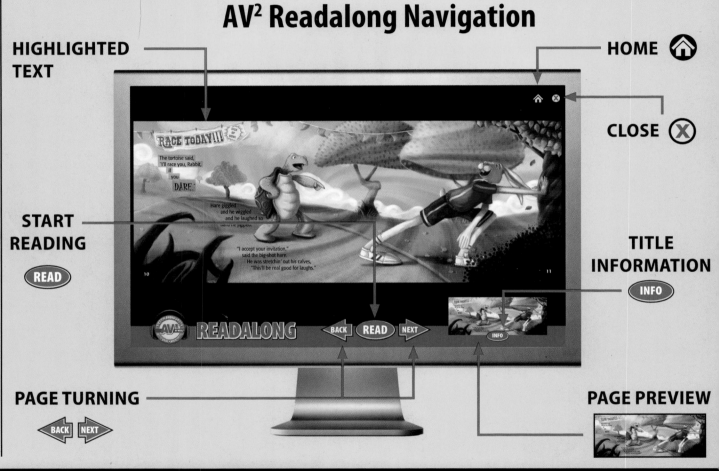

Published by AV² by Weigl
350 5ᵗʰ Avenue, 59ᵗʰ Floor New York, NY 10118
Copyright ©2013 AV² by Weigl

Printed in the United States of America in North Mankato, Minnesota
1 2 3 4 5 6 7 8 9 0 16 15 14 13 12

052012
WEP160512

Library of Congress Cataloging-in-Publication Data

Crow, Kristyn.

The really groovy story of the Tortoise and the Hare / by Kristyn Crow ; illustrated by Christina Forshay.
    p. cm.
Summary: A modern rhyme retells the events of the famous race between the boastful hare and the persevering tortoise.
ISBN 978-1-61913-128-6 (hard cover : alk. paper)
[1. Stories in rhyme. 2. Fables. 3. Folklore.] I. Forshay, Christina, ill. II. Aesop. III. Hare and the tortoise. English. IV. Title.
PZ8.3.C8858Re 2012
398.2--dc23
[E]   2012017021

For J.A.H. with love always ~ K.C.

For Chase and Ella. Love, Mama

Deep inside the city
was a hip and happy hare.
He was zippy,
sometimes lippy,
takin' taxis everywhere.

5

Way out in the country
was a tortoise calm and cool.

6

He was quite the mellow fellow
chillin' out beside the pool.

zip zap zowie...

they bumped their heads—

Ka-powie

when the tortoise met the hare at the happenin' county fair.

8

They shuffled
and they snuffled
and they felt a little ruffled.

9

RACE TODAY!!! SIGN UP NOW!

The tortoise said,
"I'll race you, Rabbit,
if
you
DARE."

Hare giggled
and he wiggled
and he laughed so
hard he jiggled.

"I accept your invitation,"
said the big-shot hare.
He was stretchin' out his calves,
"This'll be real good for laughs."

Tortoise whispered, "*Slow and steady.*"
Hare said, "Tortoise, are you ready?"

On your mark!

Yo!

Set?

You bet!

THEN GO!

13

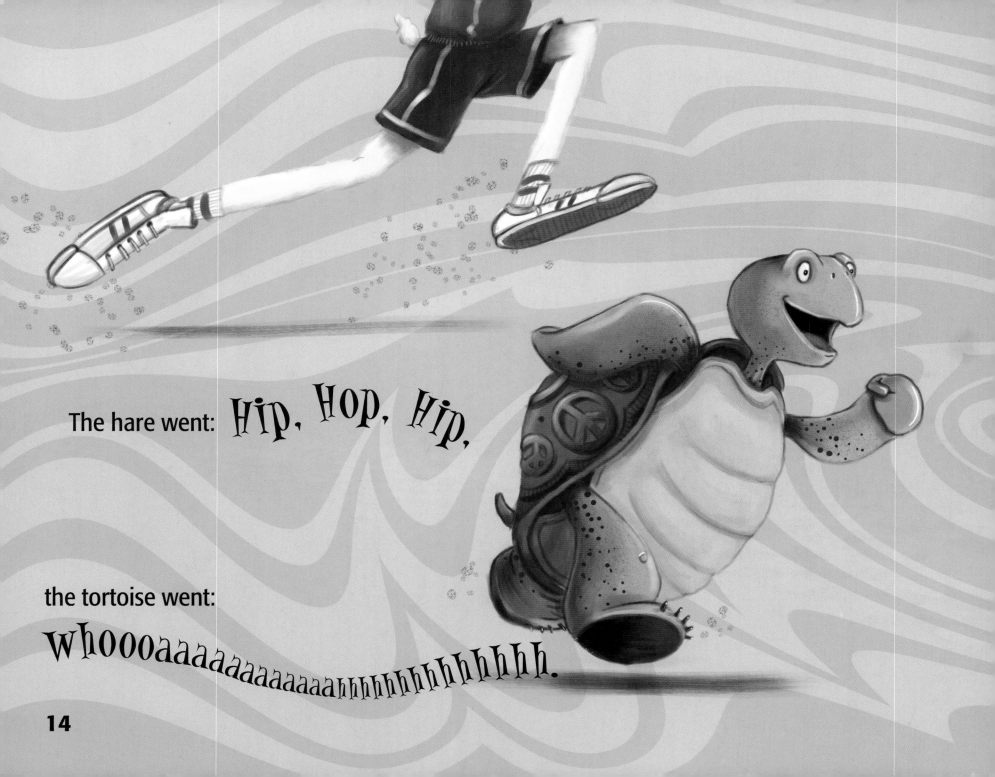

The hare went: Hip, Hop, Hip,

the tortoise went:

whooooaaaaaaaaaaaaaahhhhhhhhhhhhhh.

14

The hare went: **Zippity-zappity-zip,**

the tortoise went: **slow dee-oh dee-oh.**

Well, Hare, he really scurried
tho' he wasn't even worried
'cause he left the silly tortoise in the dust.
"I really hate to beat you but I must."

Tortoise only dallied as the crowd around them rallied— *"I'll bet Hare is gonna beat him by a*

Big **Fat** Mile."

(The tortoise kept a-strollin' with a smile).

Now, Hare, man, he grooved
and he proved it while he moved
since he fled
and he sped
and he got so far ahead…

that he hopped
and he stopped…
found a comfy place,
and flopped.

That ol' tortoise just
meandered down the track…
while his rival started
feastin' on a snack.

Hare, he slurped
and he burped
while the birds above
him chirped.

Yes, he nibbled—
even dribbled—
got a sketchpad out
and scribbled.

Then he rapped
and he tapped—
curled into a ball
and napped.

21

22

The tortoise kept-a-movin' sure and slow—
Hare was teasin', "Here's a concert as you go!"

Then he danced
and he pranced
till the crowd became entranced,
as he rocked while he squawked
making everybody shocked!

When suddenly
he realized— "ZADS!"
The tortoise nearly won!
The nervous hare, he hollered,

"Jumpin' Jive!
What have I done?"

24

So he hustled and he bustled
with his ears a little tussled—
as he raced and he chased
(since he'd *hate* to be disgraced)-

yes, he VROOMED
and he ZOOMED
while the dust around him plumed.

25

Then he swooped
ally-ooped
and he even loop-de-looped
as he slid
to a skid—
and the nervous
tortoise hid.

27

The dust cleared
as the hare
came
to
a
stop.

Then Tortoise peeked his head out with a POP!

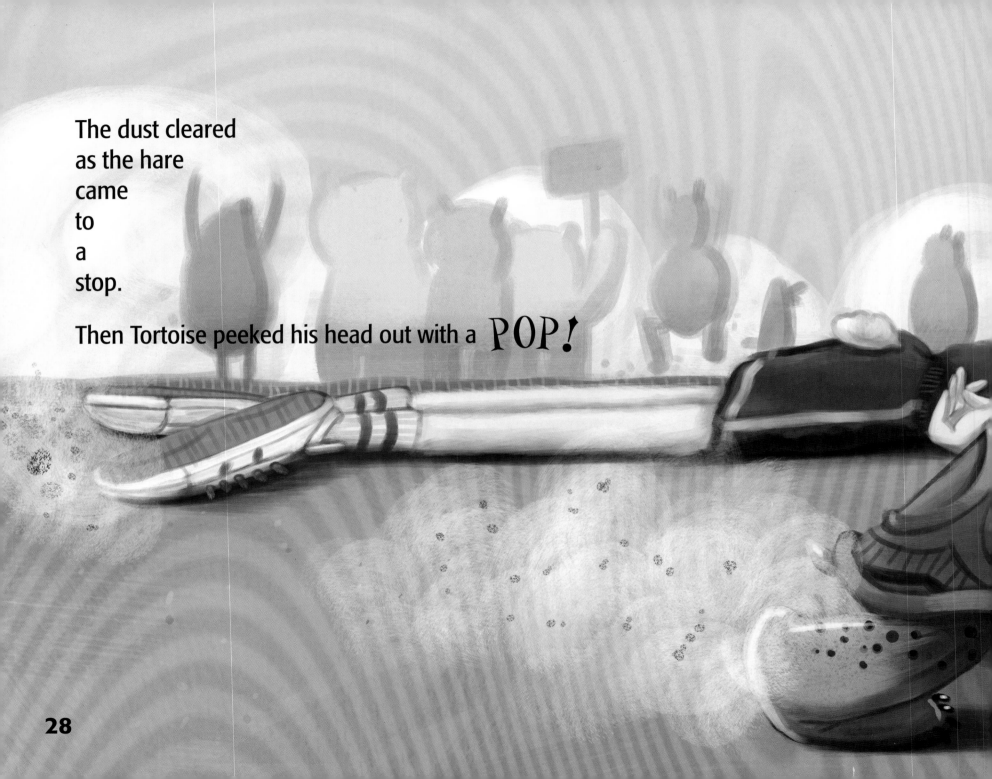

Tortoise won it by a nose!

... and that's the way our story goes.

"That was **Groovy!**
That was **Fun!**"

Hare said, *"Dude, I shoulda' won."*

30

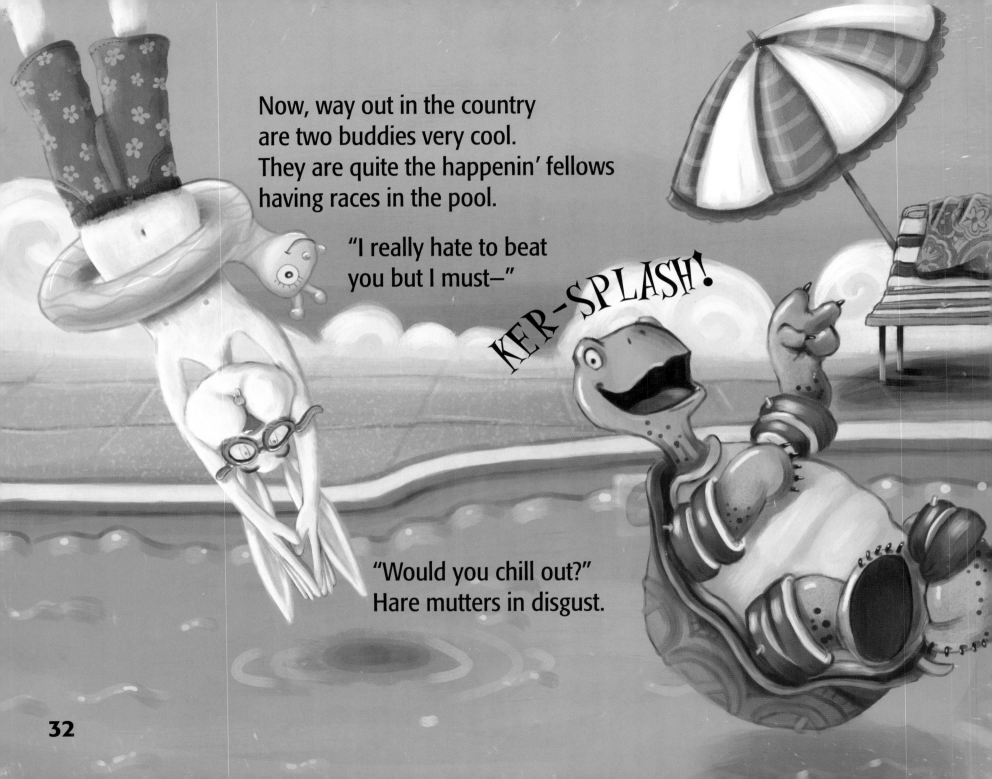

Now, way out in the country
are two buddies very cool.
They are quite the happenin' fellows
having races in the pool.

"I really hate to beat
you but I must—"

KER-SPLASH!

"Would you chill out?"
Hare mutters in disgust.